Hot Diggity Dogs

Ready, Set, Dogs!

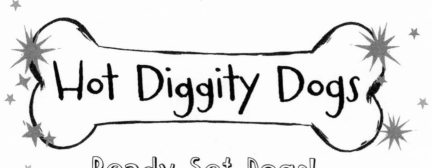

Hot Diggity Dogs

Ready, Set, Dogs!

Stephanie Calmenson & Joanna Cole
illustrated by Heather Ross

Christy Ottaviano Books

Henry Holt and Company

New York

Henry Holt and Company, LLC
Publishers since 1866
175 Fifth Avenue
New York, New York 10010
mackids.com

Library of Congress Cataloging-in-Publication Data

Calmenson, Stephanie, author.
Hot diggity dogs / Stephanie Calmenson & Joanna Cole ;
illustrated by Heather Ross. — First edition.
pages cm. — (Ready, set, dogs! ; 3)
Summary: When a new hot dog stand opens in town, dog-lovers Kate and Lucie
rush to try it out and the food is great, but the owners' dachshunds, Ketchup and Mustard,
soon disappear and it is up to the girls to save the day, while evading boys and preparing
for the Bark-in-the-Park dog competition.
ISBN 978-0-8050-9649-1 (hardback) — ISBN 978-0-8050-9650-7 (e-book)
[1. Dogs—Fiction. 2. Best friends—Fiction. 3. Friendship—Fiction. 4. Shapeshifting—Fiction.
5. Dachshunds—Fiction. 6. Humorous stories.]
I. Cole, Joanna, author. II. Ross, Heather, illustrator. III. Title.
PZ7.C136Hn 2015   [E]—dc23   2015000585

Henry Holt books may be purchased for business or promotional use. For information on
bulk purchases, please contact the Macmillan Corporate and Premium Sales Department
at (800) 221-7945 x5442 or by e-mail at specialmarkets@macmillan.com.

First Edition—2015
Printed in the United States of America by R. R. Donnelley & Sons Company,
Crawfordsville, Indiana

1 3 5 7 9 10 8 6 4 2

To Harry, my hot-diggity dachshund
—S. C.

To Gracie, who is a half-diggity dachshund
—J. C.

Contents

1. Summer Sizzles   1

2. Hot Diggity Dogs   10

3. Dogs at the Park   18

4. Bark and Bake   24

5. Runaway Hot Dogs   31

6. Be a Tree, Be a Rock   39

7. Gotcha!   44

8. Smartie Dogs   51

9. Ketchup! Mustard!   56

10. Doom and Gloom   65

11. Bark-in-the-Park   71

12. Trophies and Treats   78

Woof-Ha-Ha! Short Jokes for Long Dogs   91

Dachshunds: Many Sizes, Coats, and Colors   93

Doxies on Parade   94

Why Do Dachshunds Have Short Legs?   95

A Dachshund and a Poodle
by Stephanie Calmenson   96

Never Had a Dachshund
by Joanna Cole   98

Hot Diggity Dogs

Ready, Set, Dogs!

Summer Sizzles

Two dogs were trotting side by side down the street. They both had collars with pink dog bones hanging down.

One dog was mostly white with tan spots, tan patches around her eyes, and dark brown ears.

The other dog was shaggy, with ginger-colored fur that hung down almost to her eyes.

The dogs' tongues were hanging way out the sides of their mouths. They were both hot, hot, hot.

As they passed Didi's Bakery, they heard a voice booming from the radio. The voice belonged to Amos-on-the-Airwaves. He was Tuckertown's favorite radio personality.

"Grab your ice cubes, listeners! It's going to be a sizzling summer day!" said Amos.

"I'd love an ice cube right now," said the white-spotted dog.

"Make mine chicken-flavored!" said the shaggy ginger-colored one.

The dogs weren't yipping or barking. They were talking in words. That's because these were no ordinary dogs.

The dogs kept walking. The voice on the radio kept talking. This time the voice was coming from Bubble-Up Wash & Dry. Everyone in town listened to Amos-on-the-Airwaves.

"Remember, Bark-in-the-Park is coming soon," said Amos. "There'll be woofs, wags, and goody bags!"

The dogs stopped short. They looked at each other.

"Did he say goody bags?" said the spotted dog.

"He did," said the shaggy one. "Do you think they'll be for the dogs or for the kids?"

"It doesn't matter to us," said the first dog. "We can be either."

The dogs were just coming up to the Lucky Find Thrift Shop.

"Want to go in and look around?" said the spotted dog.

"Sure!" said the shaggy one. "But we know the rule."

A big sign in the window said NO DOGS ALLOWED. The dogs knew what they had to do.

"Let's go around to the back," said the spotted dog.

They trotted behind the shop. A minute

later, two girls were standing where the dogs had been.

One girl was Kate Farber. She had freckles that were like the white dog's tan spots. She was wearing glasses that looked a lot like the patches around the dog's eyes. Her dark brown pigtails looked like the dog's ears.

The other girl was Lucie Lopez. She had ginger-colored hair with bangs that almost covered her eyes. Her hair looked a lot like the shaggy coat of the ginger-colored dog.

The girls were both wearing I ♥ DOGS T-shirts and matching necklaces with pink dog bones. Their necklaces were a lot like the dogs' collars.

Each girl wanted a real dog of her own but couldn't have one. The girls lived next door to each other in garden apartments that had the same rule as the thrift shop: NO DOGS ALLOWED.

But something amazing had happened. Instead of *having* dogs, Kate and Lucie had found a way to *be* dogs.

It had happened one day right in the Lucky Find Thrift Shop. The girls found two great-looking necklaces with pink dog bones and went into the dressing room to try them on.

They helped each other with the clasps and turned to admire themselves.

"These look great on us!" said Lucie.

"Let's buy them!" said Kate.

"*Woofa-woof!*" they said together, and gave each other high fives.

Woofa-wow! Just as their hands touched, the necklaces lit up. There was a pop and a whoosh in the dressing room, and two dogs were staring back at them from the mirror. The girls had turned into dogs!

After a few tries, they learned how to change back and forth whenever they wanted to.

Now that they were girls again, Kate and Lucie walked to the front door of the Lucky Find.

"I saw a big box of hats delivered the other day," said Lucie. "There were even some with pink ribbons!"

"Uh-oh," said Kate, rolling her eyes. "You and ribbons are a dangerous combination."

Lucie loved ribbons and everything pink.

"Hi, Mrs. Bingly!" Kate called to the store's owner as they walked inside.

Lucie took a quick look around the shop.

"Where are the new hats with ribbons?" she asked.

"They sold really fast," said Mrs. Bingly. "Everyone loved them."

"I did, too," said Lucie, looking disappointed.

Then she saw a basket of mini stuffed dogs.

"Look how cute these are!" she said. "I like the pink one best."

Since Kate and Lucie couldn't have real dogs, they had dog pj's and slippers, dog sheets and pillowcases, dog pictures, and even dog lamps.

Lucie's room was overflowing with stuffed dogs. She also had her own library of dog books. They were everywhere. She had read every one and knew a lot about dogs.

Kate's room was neat as a pin. All her things were carefully arranged. Her collection of little glass dogs was lined up in size order.

Kate was excited when she spotted a shelf with some glass dogs on it.

"I want one of those. I like the Yorkie," she said.

"You get that, and I'll get the pink dog," said Lucie.

"Wait, we have to see if we have enough

money," said Kate, being her sensible self.

The girls checked their pockets. Things at the thrift shop usually didn't cost much, and they were happy knowing the money they spent went to charity.

"I've got enough and money left over," said Lucie.

"Me too," said Kate.

"We're lucky dogs!" said Lucie.

The girls tried to keep straight faces as they went to pay Mrs. Bingly for their treasures.

Hot Diggity Dogs

Kate and Lucie started walking toward home with their new Lucky Find dogs. Suddenly, Lucie lifted her nose and started sniffing the air.

"In case you've forgotten, you're not a dog anymore," said Kate. "You're a girl."

"I know. I'm a girl who smells hot dogs," said Lucie.

Sniff, sniff. "I smell them, too," said Kate. "Let's go!"

The girls followed their noses up the street

and around the corner. They saw a banner ahead that said GRAND OPENING. Above it was a sign that said HOT DIGGITY DOGS.

"Whoa! A new hot dog stand," said Kate. "That is so cool."

"No, it's not. It's hot!" said Lucie.

"Very funny," said Kate.

The hot dog stand really was a cool one. There were pictures of all kinds of hot dogs and a million toppings. The stand had a fence all around it. Kate and Lucie opened the gate and went in.

There were signs everywhere they looked. Kate read the first one.

" 'Please close gate,' " she said. She closed the gate.

" 'We serve healthy hot dogs,' " said Lucie, reading the next sign.

" 'Our dogs don't bite. You bite our dogs!' " read Kate.

" 'Number one award-winning hot dogs,' " read Lucie.

Kate and Lucie saw a young couple at the counter. They were both tall and thin. Their name tags said Molly and Wally. Their white caps and aprons had pictures of hot dogs all over them.

"Hi, girls!" they called. Then they pointed to each other.

"This is Wally," said the woman.

"This is Molly," said the man.

Kate and Lucie joined in. They pointed to each other.

"This is Kate," said Lucie.

"This is Lucie," said Kate.

Two little dachshunds came running out. They were short and long. Very short. Very long.

"They're hot dogs, too!" said Lucie.

"I love 'dash-hounds'!" said Kate. "They're so cute."

"We say 'dox-hunds,'" said Molly.

"Or we call them doxies," said Wally. "This is Ketchup."

He pointed at the reddish-brown one.

"This is Mustard," said Molly. She pointed at the golden one.

"May we pet them?" said Lucie.

"Sure, they're really friendly," said Molly.

"My dog books say to hold out your hand for a dog to sniff," said Lucie.

"Let's do it," Kate said.

The girls each held out a hand to one of the dachshunds.

"Don't reach over their heads," said Lucie.

"You're being pretty bossy," Kate said.

"Well, it could scare them," said Lucie.

Kate and Lucie reached from the side and gently petted the dogs' soft backs.

"Look at them wagging," said Molly. "You've got two new friends."

Kate and Lucie finished petting the doxies and looked up at the pictures of hot dogs on the menu.

"I'm getting hungry," said Kate.

"Me too," said Lucie.

"You're in the right place," Molly said.

"What kind of hot dog would you like?" asked Wally.

The girls studied the choices. Each hot dog had a number. Each topping had a letter.

"Pick one number and two letters," said Molly.

Turkey dog was 1.

Chicken was 2.

Veggie was 3.

Beef was 4.

The hot dogs came in two sizes—long and short.

Then came the toppings.

Mustard was the letter A.

Ketchup was B.

Relish was C.

Sauerkraut was D.

Crushed pineapple was E.

"E for ewww!" said Lucie.

"A pineapple hot dog? You're kidding, right?" said Kate to Molly and Wally.

"It's really good," said Wally.

"Be brave and try it," said Molly.

"Maybe next time," said Lucie. "I'll have 2 with A and B."

"I'll have 3 with B and C," said Kate.

"Long or short?" asked Wally.

"It's their first time here," said Molly. "So let's give them both long."

Kate and Lucie paid for their hot dogs. Then Wally and Molly went to work.

"Here you go!" said Wally. "A 2-A-B for you, Lucie."

"And a 3-B-C for you, Kate," said Molly.

They handed the girls their hot dogs. Kate and Lucie bit into them at the same time.

"Mine is delicious," said Lucie.

"Mine too," said Kate.

"Come back soon," said Wally.

"I hope we'll see you at Bark-in-the-Park," said Molly.

"Girls, please be sure to close the gate so the dogs can't get out," said Wally.

"We will," Lucie said.

The girls headed home, enjoying every bite of 2-A-B and 3-B-C.

Dogs at the Park

Kate and Lucie had just finished their hot dogs when they looked across the street to the park.

They saw Darleen, a girl in their class, in the dog run with her dogs, Bo and Boo.

"Want to go in?" asked Lucie.

"Definitely," said Kate. "Look how much fun Bo and Boo are having."

The girls disappeared to a spot where no one could see them and . . .

Woofa-wow! With a pop and a whoosh,
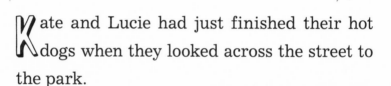

they came back out as dogs. As soon as the gate to the dog run opened, they slipped inside.

Four big dogs and three small ones hurried over to greet them. The dogs circled and sniffed to say hello.

Across the way, Darleen called, "Fetch!" Kate and Lucie wagged their tails. They raced over to join the game.

Lucie jumped up and caught the ball in the air. Boo and Bo didn't mind. Boo was big, black, and goofy-friendly. Bo was tiny, tan, and yippy-happy.

Then Kate chased Lucie, trying to get the ball from her.

"*Grrr*," said Lucie, kidding around.

She turned fast to get away from Kate. Then she ran and dropped the ball at Darleen's feet.

"Good dog!" said Darleen. "You can play with us if you want. Fetch!"

She threw the ball in the air again. This time Boo got it.

"Good dog, Boo! Maybe you'll win the fetch contest at Bark-in-the-Park," said Darleen.

After a few rounds of the game, Kate stopped and lifted her head to sniff the air.

"Do you smell what I smell?" she whispered to Lucie.

"Banana-Fandana gum!" Lucie whispered back.

That meant DJ Jackson was in the park. Sometimes they had fun with him, but usually he was one of the most annoying boys on the planet. He loved Banana-Fandana gum and always had at least three pieces in his mouth at once. He said it gave him the full flavor.

"Do you hear what I hear?" said Kate.

Thunk, thunk, thunk.

"Loud and clear," whispered Lucie.

That meant that Danny DeMarco was in the park. Sometimes they had fun with him, too, but he was the other most annoying boy on the planet. As usual, he was bouncing his basketball while he walked. *Thunk, thunk, thunk.*

"Let's go be the most annoying dogs on the planet," whispered Lucie.

"Sounds like fun," said Kate.

They left Boo, Bo, and Darleen behind and slipped out of the dog run as soon as someone opened the gate.

"There are those dogs again," said Danny.

Danny and DJ had seen them around town lots of times.

"Boy, I wish they were our dogs," said DJ.

"We should start carrying leashes just in case," said Danny.

"Yeah, just in case we can catch them," said DJ.

"In your dreams," whispered Kate to Lucie.

Kate ran up to Danny and bonked the basketball out of his reach.

"Hey!" called DJ. When his mouth opened, his gum dropped out.

Lucie stepped right in it.

"Yuck! DJ's gum is stuck on my paw," whispered Lucie, trying to pull her paw from the ground.

"So much for having fun," said Kate.

Lucie dragged the string of gum all the way back to their hiding place. *Woofa-wow!* They changed back to girls and got to work scraping the gum off Lucie's shoe.

Bark and Bake

"Hi, Moms!" the girls called when they got home.

Kate's and Lucie's moms were best friends just like Kate and Lucie.

Kate's mom baked cookies, cakes, and pies that were sold at the farmers market and at Didi's Bakery. So she was home a lot.

Lucie's mom was a teacher at the Little Apple School House. It was summer, so she was home, too.

The moms were working in the garden they had made together.

The girls could hear the radio playing through Lucie's kitchen window.

"*Yip, yip, woof!*" Amos-on-the-Airwaves was at it again.

"Don't forget to come to Bark-in-the-Park. It's for a great cause," he said. "The money we raise will go to the Tuckertown Library. We need folks to volunteer at the booths and to donate cakes, cookies, and dog treats."

"Did he say treats?" said Kate.

"He did," said Lucie. "Are you thinking what I'm thinking?"

"That we should make dog treats?" said Kate.

"Exactly," said Lucie.

"Is that okay, Mom?" asked Kate.

"Sure," said Mrs. Farber. "You can use some of our vegetables."

"That will make the treats nice and healthy," said Mrs. Lopez.

Together, they filled a basket with carrots, beans, and zucchini. Then they all went into Kate's house since Mrs. Farber had everything a baker could need.

Kate and Lucie turned on the computer to look for recipes.

"Here's one that has vegetables," said Kate. "It's called Very Veggie Doggie Treats."

"Perfect," said Lucie.

While their moms were washing the vegetables in the sink, the girls took turns reading the recipe.

"We need whole wheat flour," said Lucie.

"Two eggs," said Kate.

"And grated vegetables," said Lucie. "There's a note here that says onions are dangerous for dogs."

"No problem. No onions," said Kate.

Mrs. Farber got out the food processor while Mrs. Lopez gathered the rest of the ingredients. Kate and Lucie got out measuring cups, bowls, and spoons.

When the food processor was set up, the girls dropped in vegetables one by one.

"Okay, Mom," said Kate.

"Ready . . . set . . . ," said Lucie.

"Go!" the girls said together.

Mrs. Farber held the top and pushed the start button. The machine roared, and the girls covered their ears.

In no time, they had a bowl full of greenish veggie mush.

"Yuck," said Lucie.

"What dog will eat that?" said Kate.

"Patience, girls," said Mrs. Lopez. "They'll be delicious."

They took turns mixing everything together and rolling out the dough. Kate opened

a drawer, then she and Lucie took out the cookie cutters.

"We've got a star," said Lucie. "And a heart."

"Those are good," said Kate. "Witch's hat? Turkey? Snowman?"

"Wrong season," said Lucie. "What about this flower or the butterfly?"

"Those will work. Flower, butterfly, heart, star," said Kate.

They pressed the cookie cutters into the dough to cut out the shapes. Then they put them on the baking sheets. Mrs. Farber popped the sheets into the oven and set the timer.

Soon the kitchen started to smell great.

When the treats were done, Mrs. Lopez put

them on cooling racks. In no time they were ready for Kate and Lucie to put into bags.

"Let's make a bag for Ketchup and Mustard," said Lucie.

"Excuse me?" said Mrs. Farber. "I don't think dogs would like ketchup or mustard on their treats."

Kate and Lucie giggled.

"Those are the names of the dogs at the new hot dog stand," said Kate.

"It's called Hot Diggity Dogs," said Lucie. "I got a 2-A-B."

"I got a 3-B-C," said Kate. "It was delicious."

"What are you girls talking about?" said Mrs. Lopez.

"We'll tell you later, Mom," said Lucie. "Right now we have dog treats to deliver."

Runaway Hot Dogs

They had gone only a little way when Kate said, "These treats smell really good."

"They sure do," said Lucie. "Are you thinking what I'm thinking?"

"That we could eat a couple of these treats if we were dogs?" said Kate.

"Exactly," said Lucie. "In fact, someone should taste-test them."

"We're just the dogs to do it," said Kate.

They slipped between two houses and got

down low, putting the bag of treats on the ground.

"*Woofa-woof!*" they whispered. At the same time they gave each other high fives.

Woofa-wow! Their necklaces lit up. With a pop and a whoosh, the girls were dogs.

Kate nosed open the bag.

"One for me and one for you," she said.

They each took a treat.

"Yum! Crunchy," said Kate.

"And tasty," said Lucie.

"We'd better try one more to be sure," said Kate.

They each ate another.

"These really are delicious," said Kate.

"It's good we're dog-testing them," said Lucie. "In fact, I think we should try another."

"I think you're right," said Kate.

They put their dog noses back into the bag.

Kate ate one. Lucie ate one. Kate ate another.
Lucie ate another. Treat crumbs were flying!

When they put their noses in the bag again,
they came up empty.

"Uh-oh," said Lucie.

"We didn't leave any," said Kate.

"Shame on us," said Lucie.

"We're dogs, we couldn't help it," said Kate.

"What will we do now? What will we give Ketchup and Mustard?" said Lucie.

The dogs cocked their heads and thought. Then Kate got an idea.

"We'll give them belly rubs," she said.

"They'll love that," said Lucie. "Let's go!"

Kate and Lucie turned themselves back into girls. They put the empty treat bag in a trash can and went on to Hot Diggity Dogs.

But when they got there, they were surprised. Instead of a big sign saying GRAND OPENING, there was a big sign that said CLOSED.

"What? What happened?" said Kate.

"How could they be closed? They just opened," said Lucie.

Kate and Lucie weren't the only ones who

were surprised. People kept coming to the hot dog stand.

"The hot dogs here were great," said a young woman. "My favorite was 4-C-D."

"Mine was 3-B-C," said Kate.

Suddenly, a bunch of kids ran by.

"Come help!" they called.

"Why? What's happening?" said Lucie.

"Ketchup! Mustard!" said a girl who was out of breath.

"What about them?" said Kate.

"They're missing!" called the girl as she disappeared around the corner.

"Help us find them!" called a boy.

All the people at the hot dog stand started running in different directions.

"Here, Ketchup! Here, Mustard!" they called.

"Let's go!" said Lucie.

They ran down one street and up another.

There were people everywhere looking for the missing dogs.

Up ahead, they saw two white hats with hot dogs on them. It was Wally and Molly.

"Ketchup and Mustard are missing!" said Molly.

"We have to find them!" said Wally.

"We know! We're looking, too," said Kate.

"What happened?" said Lucie.

"Someone left the gate open," said Molly. She started to cry.

"Thanks for helping us," said Wally, putting his arm around Molly.

Molly and Wally ran down one street. Kate and Lucie raced up another. Wherever they went, there were lots of people calling for Ketchup and Mustard.

"You know what I'm thinking?" said Kate.

"That everyone's looking in the same place?" said Lucie.

"That's right. Those dogs could be on the other side of town by now," said Kate.

"We should go home and make 'lost dog' signs," said Lucie.

"Let's hurry!" said Kate.

The girls ran all the way home.

Be a Tree, Be a Rock

At Lucie's house, the girls got out some paper and markers. They drew a reddish-brown dachshund and a golden one.

"What should we say?" said Lucie.

"LOST!" said Kate. "And we have to put their names and a phone number."

They looked up the phone number for Hot Diggity Dogs. They wrote everything in big letters.

"How about some sparkles?" said Lucie.

"This is a sign, not a work of art," said Kate, being her usual sensible self.

"Stickers?" said Lucie.

"No! We have to hurry. We need to make copies, put up the signs, and find the dogs!" said Kate.

"You're right," said Lucie.

They made two dozen copies on Lucie's mom's printer. Then they grabbed a roll of tape and ran out to put up their signs.

"Where do we start?" said Kate.

"Let's put one right here," said Lucie.

They put the first sign on a big oak tree near their street.

"That's a pretty great sign," said Lucie, admiring their work.

Kate rolled her eyes.

"Stop with the sign," she said. "We have to hurry!"

They posted four signs on every block,

two on each side. As they went, they called, "Ketchup! Mustard!"

They heard two dogs bark.

"Maybe it's them!" said Kate.

"Ketchup! Mustard!" they called again.

Two dogs came charging from a backyard. One was golden like mustard and the other was reddish-brown like ketchup. But they weren't little like the doxies. They were enormous!

"Ahhhhh!" yelled Kate.

Lucie stayed quiet and stood perfectly still.

"What are you doing? Let's run," said Kate.

"Speak softly and do not move," said Lucie gently. "My dog books say to be a rock or a tree with no branches if you're scared of a dog."

Kate stood like a tree. She was staring at the dogs.

"Don't look at them," said Lucie. "Trees and rocks don't stare."

The dogs stopped running and stood barking at Kate and Lucie.

A man came out onto the porch of the house.

"Ketchup! Mustard! Come!" he said.

The dogs turned and ran to him.

"I can't believe it!" Kate whispered to Lucie. "Those huge dogs have the same names as the little doxies."

"My dogs are noisy, but they won't hurt you," said the man. "By the way, why were you calling their names?"

"Two little dachshunds named Ketchup and Mustard are lost," said Lucie.

"If you see them, call the number on the sign," said Kate.

"I sure will," said the man as he took his dogs inside.

Gotcha!

Kate and Lucie kept hanging up their signs. Finally, they had none left.

"Now what do we do?" said Kate. "Where can we find those doxies?"

"Well, where would we go if we were dogs?" said Lucie.

"That's it!" said Kate. "We can *be* dogs to *find* dogs."

"We can track them down with our super dog noses," said Lucie. "Let's do it!"

They found a spot to hide. They said

"*Woofa-woof!*" and gave each other high fives. In a flash, they were dogs.

"Let's look in places where there aren't any signs," said Kate.

"Follow me!" said Lucie. She ran to a new part of town.

Suddenly, Lucie stopped. She lifted her nose in the air and sniffed. So did Kate.

"I don't smell the dogs, do you?" said Lucie.

"No, but there's a scary scent of Banana-Fandana gum!" said Kate.

At that very second, Danny reached out from behind a bush and grabbed Kate's collar. DJ reached from the other side and grabbed Lucie's.

"Gotcha!" said DJ.

"Finally!" said Danny.

They took leashes from their pockets and clipped them onto Kate's and Lucie's collars.

"*Woof! Woof!*" barked Kate and Lucie.

They looked at each other with wild, wide eyes.

Danny had Kate on one side. DJ had Lucie on the other.

"It's good we got these just-in-case leashes," said DJ.

"Yeah, just in case we saw these dogs again," said Danny. "Now we have dogs for Bark-in-the-Park."

Kate and Lucie couldn't believe what was happening. They tucked their tails between their legs.

"Let's take them home!" said DJ.

They started pulling the dogs along.

"Do not take another step," Lucie whispered to Kate.

The dogs stopped.

"Sit!" Kate whispered back to Lucie.

The dogs sat. The boys pulled. The collars dug into Kate's and Lucie's necks.

"That hurts," whispered Kate.

"*Grrr*," Lucie growled loudly.

"These dogs aren't as friendly as we thought," said Danny.

"You wouldn't be friendly either if someone was tugging on your neck," Kate whispered to Lucie.

Unfortunately, the boys pulled harder.

"We have to escape. We have to find Ketchup and Mustard," Lucie whispered.

Kate and Lucie kept pulling, but the boys pulled harder.

Finally, the dogs gave up and went along.

"Let's name them," said Danny.

"Ugh! We already have names," whispered Kate.

"They don't know that," answered Lucie.

"They're girl dogs," said Danny. "I guess we have to give them girly names."

"No way!" said DJ. "I'm naming mine Fang."

Lucie yelped.

"You're next," she whispered to Kate.

"Mine's going to be Spot," said Danny.

"Very original," said Lucie, looking at Kate's tan spots.

They turned down Danny and DJ's street. It was Darleen's street, too. Her house was right between theirs.

The next thing they knew, Kate and Lucie were in Danny's backyard.

"Too bad Darleen's not around. We could show her our new dogs," said Danny.

"That's okay. We'll train them first, then show her," said DJ.

"Train us? They've got to be kidding," whispered Lucie.

"DJ!" his dad called from DJ's yard. "Come help me in the basement."

"Coming, Dad!" DJ called. Then he told Danny, "I'll be right back."

DJ pulled on Lucie's leash.

"Let's go, Fang," he said.

Lucie turned to Kate, looking for help.

"*A-woo-woo-woo!*" she howled.

"*A-woo-woo-woo!*" Kate howled back. She tried to follow, but Danny held on tight.

Kate and Lucie were being separated, and there was nothing they could do to stop it.

Smartie Dogs

DJ tied Lucie to a tree in his yard and went inside.

Danny tied Kate to a tree in his yard and said, "Stay here. I'm going in to get you a bowl of water."

Well, I can't exactly go anywhere, thought Kate. *But I am thirsty.*

As soon as Danny was gone, Kate called to Lucie, "Now what are we going to do?"

"What *can* we do?" said Lucie. "We're prisoners!"

"We need to be girls again," said Kate.

"We need to be close enough for high fives," said Lucie.

"How are we going to get free?" said Kate. "Are we strong enough to pull these trees down?"

They tried pulling.

"Ouch, my neck! I hate this collar," said Lucie.

"I hate these leashes," said Kate. "Hey, let's try chewing through them."

"Good idea!" said Lucie.

They started chewing. But they didn't get very far before Danny came out with the bowl of water.

Then DJ came out, too. He untied Lucie and walked her back to Danny's yard. He held on to her leash as the two dogs lapped up the water.

"Okay, now it's training time," said DJ. "Fang, sit!"

"Ha! Watch this," whispered Lucie.

Lucie stood up on her hind legs.

"Your dog is really dumb. Watch Spot do it," said Danny, untying Kate from the tree. "Spot, sit!"

Kate lay down and rolled over.

"Your dog's brilliant," said DJ. "Fang, come!"

Lucie sat.

"These dogs are useless," said DJ.

"No, they're not," said Danny. "Listen and learn. Spot, speak!"

Kate gave him the silent treatment.

"Dog training is harder than I thought," said Danny.

"Maybe we have to give them treats," said DJ.

"Good idea," said Danny. "I've got some Chompy Chips inside."

The boys tied the dogs to the tree.

"We'll be right back," said DJ. "Don't go anywhere."

"Yeah, right," whispered Kate.

"We like those chips, but not enough to stick around for," whispered Lucie.

Danny and DJ disappeared inside the house.

"Thank goodness they tied us to the same tree," said Lucie.

"Ready . . . ," said Kate.

"Set . . . ," said Lucie.

Kate and Lucie tapped their paws together and said, *Woofa-woof!*

Woofa-wow! The dog bones on their collars lit up. With a pop and a whoosh, they were girls again!

"Hurry!" said Kate. "We've got to get out

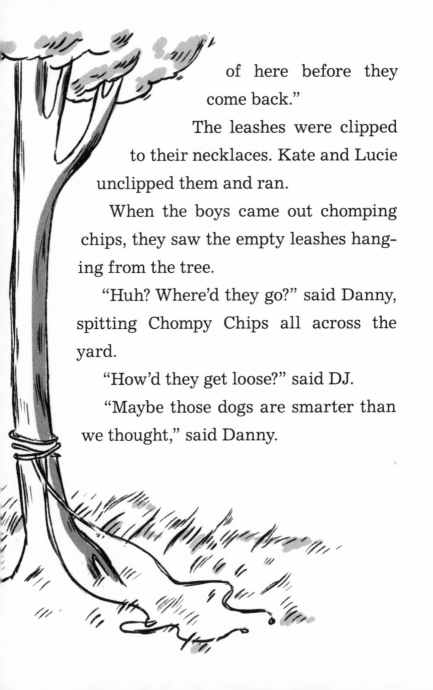

of here before they come back."

The leashes were clipped to their necklaces. Kate and Lucie unclipped them and ran.

When the boys came out chomping chips, they saw the empty leashes hanging from the tree.

"Huh? Where'd they go?" said Danny, spitting Chompy Chips all across the yard.

"How'd they get loose?" said DJ.

"Maybe those dogs are smarter than we thought," said Danny.

Ketchup! Mustard!

Kate and Lucie raced away from Danny's yard.

"Phew! That was a close one," said Lucie.

"Come on, we've got to find Ketchup and Mustard," said Kate.

"Dogs follow their noses. And their stomachs," said Lucie.

"Maybe they went to the Dumpster behind Patty's Pizza," said Kate.

"Yeah, maybe there'll be some pizza crusts there," said Lucie.

Kate rolled her eyes.

"Stop grossing me out," she said. "You're not a dog now."

They ran to the Dumpster. They didn't see the doxies.

"Where should we look next?" said Lucie.

"We haven't tried the farmers market yet," said Kate.

"You're right," said Lucie. "Let's go there now."

Kate and Lucie hurried to the market. They saw apples, corn, squash, carrots, even some of Mrs. Farber's pies. But they didn't see any doxies.

Then they passed the bathrooms.

"Maybe they're in here," said Kate. "I have to go anyway."

"Me too," said Lucie.

They went inside and looked under the stalls. They couldn't believe their eyes.

"It's Ketchup!" shouted Lucie.

"Ketchup, come!" called Kate.

But when the door opened, a mother came out with her little girl. The girl's pull-toy looked just like a doxie.

"His name is Noodle," said the girl.

"He's very cute," said Kate.

"But he's not Ketchup," Lucie whispered.

Kate and Lucie finished in the bathroom and went back out.

"What if someone found Ketchup and Mustard already?" said Kate. "We should check in at the hot dog stand."

They left the farmers market and were on their way to Hot Diggity Dogs. They were just coming up to the post office when Lucie said, "Do you see what I see?"

"Where?" said Kate.

"Under that mailbox," said Lucie. "Those two tails sticking out."

The girls got closer and bent down.

"It's Ketchup!" said Lucie.

"And Mustard!" said Kate.

The dogs got startled. They scooted out the other side of the mailbox and ran down the street.

The doxies passed so close to Well-Bee's

Drugstore, they made the automatic doors open. The dogs ran in.

By the time Kate and Lucie got inside, Ketchup and Mustard were nowhere in sight. The girls hurried up one aisle and down another.

In the first aisle, Lucie couldn't help noticing a display of nail polish.

"I could use some of that Pretty-in-Pink," said Lucie.

"I am not listening," said Kate, running into the food aisle.

"Ooh, look! Chompy Chips!" said Lucie.

"We're not here to eat," said Kate, running into the greeting card aisle.

Lucie was right behind. She couldn't resist opening a card that had six dancing chickens on the front. It turned out to be a musical card. When she opened it, it played "Old MacDonald Had a Farm."

"*Ee-i-ee-i-o!*" sang Lucie.

"This is not the way to find those dogs," said Kate.

She led the way up the next aisle.

"Oh, good, the pet supplies are here," said Lucie.

"Look! So are the dogs," said Kate. "Down there!"

On the bottom shelf was a row of comfy dog beds. Ketchup was curled up on a fleecy one shaped like a bedroom slipper. Mustard was resting his head on the arm of a cute little dog sofa.

"Ketchup!" screeched Kate.

"Mustard!" screeched Lucie.

They had never seen dogs move so fast.

"Uh-oh. We scared them again," said Kate.

"Follow those dogs!" said Lucie.

They followed them into the vitamin aisle. Right in the center were three tall towers of vitamins. The first one had bottles of vitamin B. The second was C. The third was D.

The doxies slid straight into the vitamin B tower. The tower trembled and the bottles went flying. Vitamin B flew into C. Vitamin C flew into D. Soon all three towers had fallen, and the floor was carpeted with vitamins.

The two little dogs jumped up.

Mustard landed in Kate's arms.

Ketchup landed in Lucie's arms.

The manager came running.

"Give me strength!" he called when he saw all the bottles on the floor. He reached for some vitamin C.

"Get those dogs out of here!" the manager shouted.

The girls were already running toward the exit.

"Sorry!" Kate called over her shoulder.

"We'd stay and help clean up," called Lucie. "But we've got lost dogs to return."

"Oh my! It's those lost dachshunds," said one customer.

"What good girls you are for rescuing them," said another.

"Get those dogs home fast," said a third.

The girls headed straight to Hot Diggity Dogs, carrying the doxies.

When Molly and Wally saw them coming, they threw out their arms and ran to meet them.

"Thank you! Thank you!" they said to Kate and Lucie. "Where did you find them?"

As Kate and Lucie told them the story, Wally and Molly fixed them thank-you hot dogs—their favorites, 2-A-B and 3-B-C. Yum!

10

Doom and Gloom

The morning of Bark-in-the-Park, Kate and Lucie set out to deliver their Very Veggie Doggie Treats. The booths were being set up and everyone was busy.

As the girls got near the basketball court, Lucie said, "Do you see who I see?"

"You mean Danny and DJ sitting on that bench?" said Kate.

"That would be it," said Lucie. "Do you *not* smell what I don't smell?"

"You mean no Banana-Fandana?" said Kate.

"That's right. DJ's not chewing his gum," said Lucie.

"Do you *not* hear what I don't hear?" said Kate.

"You mean no thunking?" said Lucie.

"That would be it. Danny's not bouncing his basketball," said Kate.

"Why are they just sitting and not playing?" said Lucie.

"Those boys must be seriously ill," said Kate.

They heard DJ talking and went a little closer.

"I wish we had dogs for Bark-in-the-Park," said DJ.

"We won't get to do anything fun without dogs," said Danny.

"If I had Fang, I'd win a prize for sure," said DJ.

"If I had Spot, I'd win one, too," said Danny.

"Yeah, but we don't have dogs," said DJ.

"You guys should change your names," said Lucie.

The boys jumped up.

"Your names should be Doom and Gloom," she said.

"What are you goofy girls doing here?" said Danny.

"Listening to you goofy boys," said Kate.

"We don't have dogs either," said Lucie. "But you don't see us moping around."

As soon as she said it, Kate and Lucie both realized something. They were sad, too, because they didn't have dogs to show off at Bark-in-the-Park.

All four kids sat down on the bench and felt sorry for themselves.

"We may as well practice sitting here," said Lucie.

"That's what we'll be doing when the events begin," said Danny.

"Just watching," said Kate.

"Yeah, watching everyone else have fun," said DJ.

They sat kicking their heels against the park bench.

"This is really depressing," said Kate.

"No kidding," said Lucie.

They sat for a while longer.

Suddenly, Kate stood up.

"I'm finished being depressed," she said.

"So am I," said Lucie. She stood up, too.

"We're going to deliver these dog treats," said Kate.

"We made them ourselves," said Lucie. "They're delicious."

"How would you know?" said Danny. "Did you eat them?"

"Well . . . ," said Kate and Lucie together.

"You girls are the goofiest," said DJ.

"Not as goofy as you, wasting the morning sitting on a bench," said Lucie as they walked off.

"Those boys are pitiful," said Kate.

"I feel sorry for them," Lucie said. "I can't believe I actually said that."

"I feel sorry for them, too," said Kate.

Kate and Lucie looked at each other.

"Are you thinking what I'm thinking?" said Kate.

"That we could help Danny and DJ?" said Lucie.

"That we could be their dogs for Bark-in-the-Park?" said Kate.

"Yes," said Lucie.

"No," said Kate.

"Maybe," said Lucie.

"It would be pretty horrible," said Kate. "We might even throw up."

"Then it will be Barf-in-the-Park!" said Lucie.

"Very funny," said Kate.

The girls went off with their dog-bone necklaces twinkling in the sun.

Bark-in-the-Park

The far end of the park was closed off with a big banner that said BARK-IN-THE-PARK.

The girls passed the dog-toy booth and the ring-toss game. They waved to Molly and Wally at the Hot Diggity Dogs booth and said hello to Mrs. Bingly at the Lucky Find table.

Then they dropped off their treats at the dog treat booth.

Up on the main stage, Amos-on-the-Airwaves

was howling into a microphone. He sounded like a cross between Amos and a hound dog.

"A-*woo*, listeners, *a-woo*! Welcome to Bark-in-the-Park!" he said. "Dogs, children, walruses . . . oops! No walruses."

Right under the stage, a red velvet curtain was hanging down. It was the perfect hiding place. Kate and Lucie ducked under and, with a pop and a whoosh, they came out as dogs.

"Let's go find Danny and DJ," said Lucie.

"I hope they're not still sitting on that bench," said Kate.

They weren't. The bench was empty. Across the way, there was a dog Frisbee match. Danny and DJ were watching and looking mopey.

"Yoo-hoo, boy-oys!" Lucie said under her breath as she trotted over to Danny and DJ.

"Happy Bark-in-the-Park day!" Kate whispered to Lucie, wagging her tail high.

Seconds later, Lucie grabbed DJ's shorts cuff with her teeth and tugged.

DJ turned around and said, "Fang! You're back!"

Kate jumped up on Danny, almost knocking him down.

"Hi, Spot!" said Danny.

Without missing a beat, the boys said, "Leashes!"

They pulled out their just-in-case leashes and clipped them onto the dogs' collars.

"Yes! We've got our dogs!" said Danny.

"The best dogs at the park!" said DJ.

Danny and DJ tapped their fists together. Kate and Lucie bumped their rumps.

"Come on over, dog lovers," said Amos into his microphone. "It's time for the obedience trials!"

"Why bother? We can't win that," said DJ.

"Yeah, training them didn't work out very well," said Danny.

"All we did was train them to disappear," said DJ.

"You're right, it's hopeless," said Danny. "Let's go play ring toss."

Kate and Lucie looked at each other.

"Now's our chance," whispered Lucie. "Let's go for the prize."

"We'll do everything perfectly," Kate whispered back. "The boys will faint."

"Then we'll have to be rescue dogs," said Lucie.

The boys pulled on the leashes. They were going to the ring-toss booth. Kate and Lucie pulled the other way. They were going to the obedience trials.

The dogs pulled. The boys pulled. The dogs won.

"We may as well see where they want to go," said DJ.

Kate and Lucie pulled them into the obedience ring. The trials were just beginning.

Trophies and Treats

"Dog handlers, have your dogs sit!" Amos called.

Before the boys could say a word, Kate and Lucie sat.

Danny's and DJ's mouths dropped open.

"Leave your dogs and tell them to stay," said Amos.

"Should we try it?" said DJ.

"Why not?" said Danny.

The boys stepped away.

"Stay!" they said.

Kate and Lucie sat as still as statues.

"Wow! I guess we trained them after all," said DJ, looking proud.

"Now, ask your dogs to roll over," said Amos.

Kate rolled left. Lucie rolled right.

Amos added a few more commands. Paw, please. Speak! Don't touch.

Kate and Lucie aced every one. Then they looked at each other.

"Woof?" said Lucie.

"Woof!" said Kate.

Kate and Lucie popped up, stood on their hind legs, and began to dance. They loved to dance, even when they were dogs.

Step, step, circle. Paws tap-tap. Right kick, left kick. Jump, jump, spin!

The crowd stopped and stared.

"Those are our dogs!" called Danny.

"Yep, we trained them!" said DJ.

Kate and Lucie finished their dance with backward flips. The crowd roared!

Danny and DJ each took a bow.

"I'm glad they're not mopey anymore," said Kate.

It was no surprise when Amos announced the winners.

"Boys, bring your amazing dancing dogs up to the stage for trophies and treats!" he said.

"Good job, Spot!" said Danny. "Let's go get our prize!"

"You're the greatest, Fang!" said DJ.

Amos handed the boys shiny silver trophy cups. Fang and Spot got star-shaped treats.

"These smell familiar," whispered Lucie.

"Of course they do. We made them," Kate whispered back.

Danny and DJ thanked Amos and left the trophies with him to pick up later.

"There's free dogsitting at the dog run," said Amos. "You can drop off your dogs, then have a great time at Bark-in-the-Park."

Danny and DJ left Spot and Fang in the run, then looked at all the rides and games. They spotted Darleen waiting in line for the Rocket Ride.

"Let's go on that," said DJ.

"Sounds good," said Danny.

The boys ran off toward the ride. Kate and Lucie wanted to follow. But not as dogs. They wanted to be girls again. They wanted to go on the ride, too.

As soon as the gate of the dog run opened, they slipped out and went back to their hiding place under the stage.

Woofa-wow! Kate and Lucie came out as girls and raced to the Rocket Ride. Danny and

DJ were next in line. Darleen was behind them.

"Hi, Kate. Hi, Lucie," Darleen said.

"Want to go in a rocket with us?" said Kate.

"Sure," said Darleen.

Danny and DJ turned around.

"Where have you goofy girls been?" Danny said to Kate and Lucie.

"You missed it!" said DJ.

"We got trophies!" said Danny.

Just then, it was their turn to go on the ride. Danny and DJ got into a green rocket. Kate, Lucie, and Darleen climbed into the red rocket in front of them.

"Don't pull my hair," Kate said to Danny.

"Don't kick my seat," Lucie said to DJ.

The boys rolled their eyes as the rockets started up. Round and round. Higher and higher. Faster and faster. It was a blast!

When the ride was over, Kate, Lucie, and Darleen got out. But the boys stayed.

"We're going again," said Danny.

"I can't," said Darleen, looking at her watch. "I've got to get home."

The kids said good-bye to Darleen.

"I don't want to go again either," said Lucie. "I'm hungry."

"I'm thirsty," Kate said to Lucie. "Ready for Hot Diggity Dogs?"

"Ready!" said Lucie. "Let's *get* hot dogs and *pet* hot dogs."

When they got to the stand, Ketchup and Mustard ran up to them, wagging their tails. The girls stopped to give them belly rubs, then joined the line.

"It's time," said Kate.

"Time for what?" said Lucie.

"Time to be brave and try the pineapple hot dog," said Kate.

"You mean the E for *ewww* kind?" said Lucie.

"They're going to be E for *excellent*," said Kate.

They ordered the pineapple hot dogs and pink lemonade.

While Molly and Wally made the hot dogs and poured the lemonade, they couldn't stop thanking Kate and Lucie for finding the doxies.

The girls got their hot dogs, then went to a picnic table and sat down.

"Ready . . . ," said Lucie.

"Set . . . ," said Kate.

"Bite!" they said together.

The hot dogs really were E for *excellent*!

They were just finishing their lemonade when they heard Amos bark, "*Yip, yip, woof!* Hurry over to the arts and crafts booth, kids! Get your dog ears. Get your dog whiskers!"

"Let's go," said Kate.

Kate picked out floppy ears. She decided to go wild and painted them purple with green stripes. Of course, Lucie painted hers pink. She added purple polka dots, too.

Then they went to the face-painting line to get their whiskers. The girl in the booth painted ginger whiskers on Lucie and brown whiskers on Kate.

"You two make great-looking dogs," she said.

"Thanks," said Kate and Lucie, trying not to laugh.

"This is so cool," said Lucie as they left the booth.

"No kidding," said Kate. "We can be girls. We can be dogs. We can be girls who look like dogs!"

Then, because they love to rhyme and they love to sing, Kate and Lucie made up a Bark-in-the-Park song.

> *When we're girls, we make treats.*
> *When we're dogs, we do tricks.*
> *When we're girls, we love rides.*
> *When we're dogs, we chew sticks.*
> *And we bark, bark, bark*
> *In the park, park, park!*

"Woof! Woof!" said Kate and Lucie together.

And they walked off with their pink dog-bone necklaces twinkling in the sun.

THE END

If you love dachshunds,
wag your tail and
turn the page.

Woof-Ha-Ha!
Short Jokes for Long Dogs

What's the best place to park a dachshund?

In a barking lot.

How do you keep a dachshund from barking in your back yard?

Put him in your front yard.

Seven dachshunds were sharing one umbrella and not one of them got wet. How did that happen?

It wasn't raining.

Why isn't a dachshund's nose ever twelve inches long?

Because then it would be a foot.

What should you do with a blue dachshund?

Cheer her up.

What time is it when five dachshunds are chasing a cat down the street?

Five after one.

Dachshunds: Many Sizes, Coats, and Colors

Dachshunds come in standard, mini, and tweenie sizes.

Their coats can be smooth, long-haired, or wire-haired.

There are many different colors, such as black-and-tan, reddish brown, chocolate, golden, and cream.

Their coats may be solid-colored, dappled, spotted, and more.

Doxies on Parade

When you're a doxie, dressing up isn't just for Halloween. There are also dachshund parades. Hot dog costumes—with ketchup or mustard—are favorites.

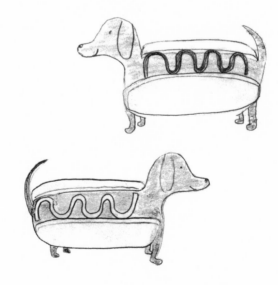

Drawing by Stephanie Calmenson

Why Do Dachshunds Have Short Legs?

Dachshunds were originally bred in Germany as hunters. Their job was to follow badgers into underground burrows. The shorter a dog's legs were, the easier it was for the dog to get into the burrow—and to get out again!

So breeders chose the dogs with the shortest legs to breed. After a while, all doxies had short legs.

A Dachshund and a Poodle

by Stephanie Calmenson

When I was a kid, I wasn't able to have a real dog. So instead I had thirteen stuffed dogs lined up along the side of my bed. One of them was a dachshund. Next to him, I had a poodle. I had hoped they would become very good friends.

Now I have a real, live dachshund named Harry. I thought about getting a poodle for Harry. But I didn't have to. My friend Carmen Gonzalez, who lives across the street, adopted a poodle named Jeeter. He and Harry liked each other right away.

Almost every afternoon, the four of us walk together. Most times, our walks are planned. But sometimes, if I'm outside with Harry and he barks, Jeeter will hear him and start racing in circles around his apartment. Carmen says it's his happy dance that means, "Take me out! Take me out!" And so she does.

The four of us walk to the park. Harry chases squirrels. Jeeter chases Harry. Harry barks at the squirrels. Jeeter barks to join the game. They have so much fun!

When Carmen travels, Jeeter stays with us. On those nights, I have two real dogs curled up in their beds next to mine—a dachshund and a poodle, who are very good friends.

Never Had a Dachshund

by Joanna Cole

I've had five dogs in my life, but never a dachshund. My grandchildren, Annabelle and William, however, have Gracie, who's a cross between a dachshund and a Chihuahua. That kind of dog is called a Chiweenie.

Like a dachshund, Gracie's snout is long and so is her body. But her legs aren't as short as a dachshund's.

Gracie was a rescue dog and was very scared when she first arrived. She was so skinny, you could see every bone in her spine right through her fur. She also has a very thin coat that doesn't do much to keep her warm. So she was very shivery.

Now, though, Gracie is happy, sleek, and not scared at all. She still shivers sometimes, but she has a bright orange sweater, a blue coat with a hood, and several fleecy blankets to keep her warm.

She loves to go for walks and even rides in a bicycle basket. When the bike goes fast, her floppy ears blow back and look like wings in the wind.

Annabelle says that when Gracie yawns, she makes a sound like a rubber ducky squeaking. And William says she's not a Chiweenie, she's a Chi-winky-dink!

Whatever else she is, Gracie is a sweetie and a welcome addition to our family.

About the Authors

Carlos Chiossone

Annabelle Helms

Stephanie Calmenson and **Joanna Cole** are friends who have written many children's books.

Stephanie is the author of such favorites as *Dinner at the Panda Palace*; *Late for School!*; *Ollie's School Day*; and books about her dogs, including *May I Pet Your Dog?*, which stars her dachshund, Harry.

Joanna, author of a wide range of highly acclaimed books, including *Bony-Legs*; *Hungry, Hungry Sharks*; and *How You Were*

Born, is best known for her popular Magic School Bus series.

Because they are such good friends, the authors have written and edited quite a few books as a team, the latest being the Ready, Set, Dogs! series.

Stephanie lives in New York City with her husband, Mark, and their dog, Harry.

Joanna lives in Iowa with her husband, Phil, and their two guinea pigs, Pepper and Paprika.